Easter Treat

EASTER
TREAT

WRITTEN AND ILLUSTRATED BY

Roger Duvoisin

Alfred A. Knopf · New York

L. C. catalog card number: 54-5308

**THIS IS A BORZOI BOOK,
PUBLISHED BY ALFRED A. KNOPF, INC.**

It was springtime; nearly Easter.

Santa Claus stood at the window of his warm igloo at the North Pole and beheld the snow-covered plain which spread far out to meet the grey sky.

"My dear," said Santa to Mrs. Santa, "sometimes I grow tired of icy winds and snowflakes. I want to take a vacation from my toy-making. I want to go and see the spring flowers."

"But Santa," said Mrs. Santa, "you cannot show yourself when it isn't Christmas! What will people think?"

"Oh, I know," sang Santa,

"My red coat and my white beard,
Christmas trees and Poinsettias,
plum puddings and gay wrappings,

only come in wintertime when the snow is on the ground; when the trees are bare and black; when the birds forget to sing. Well, this spring I want to see the daffodils and the tulips bloom; hear the birds sing among the lilac buds; walk along streets bright with spring sun."

"I think you are foolish," scolded Mrs. Santa. "How funny you will look with your red coat when people have long forgotten about Christmas. You may be arrested."

"Ah," smiled Santa, "but I will go IN-COG-NI-TO which means no one will know who I am. I will dress like a tourist and leave my red suit here in the closet."

Santa picked the mail-order catalog from a shelf and wrote an order for a complete new outfit for his trip.

When the package came, he was as happy as a child at Christmas.

He unwrapped an elegant felt hat,

a well-creased pair of slacks with yellow suspenders,

a beautiful plaid tweed coat,
a white shirt, a bow tie with polka dots, so pretty that Santa
thought it was a shame that his beard covered it,

a smart pair of shiny shoes,
and an umbrella for the spring rains.
"You look very handsome!" cried Mrs. Santa with pride.

The next day Santa harnessed his reindeer and flew to the nearest airport. He could not ride his sleigh all the way to the warmer country because there was no more snow to land on.

Then he boarded a plane which flew him to the big city.

How different the city looked at Eastertime!

"It's a new city," thought Santa. "Fresh and gay and filled with flowers."

He sat in the park in the warm sun and watched the robins hop on the green lawn and the sparrows gather twigs for their nests.

He strolled through the streets where flower carts replaced the Christmas tree stands he had seen on his last trip; where the store windows were decorated with tulips, daffodils, and forsythia, with big sugar Easter eggs, with white rabbits and cotton chicks.

He admired the pretty women who had put away their fur coats and wore light straw hats and bright dresses. And he nodded at the men who walked lightly with smiles on their faces.

Santa wanted to look like Easter, too. So he bought a fresh daffodil to stick in his lapel. And he walked along the street feeling warm and happy.

He even whistled *Jingle Bells!* But he stopped short because people began to stare at him. *Jingle Bells* at Eastertime!

"Oh, well," thought Santa, "I am really incognito. No one will know me."

When he turned the corner, Santa found himself in a street full of children playing jump rope and marbles.

As he stood there, watching, a small girl came to him dancing and singing,

> *"Oh, see the little old man.*
> *He snatched Santa's white beard;*
> *he stole Santa's red nose;*
> *and wears his gay twinkle."*

Santa was surprised. He wanted to travel incognito, but he did not want to be taken for a thief.

"You are quite wrong, my child," he said. "I stole nothing from Santa Claus."

But more children came and formed a ring around Santa. They danced and sang,

> *"Yes you did,*
> *yes you did.*
> *His white beard,*
> *his red nose,*
> *his gay twinkle,*
> *you stole from dear Santa."*

Santa was so astonished now that he even forgot he didn't want anyone to know who he was.

> *"But, my children," he cried,*
> *"this is MY white beard,*
> *this is MY red nose*
> *this is MY gay twinkle.*
> *I AM SANTA CLAUS!"*

The children only laughed.

> *"No you aren't,*
> *no you aren't.*
> *Santa has big black boots.*
> *Santa has a red coat.*
> *Santa has a red cap.*
> *Santa never comes when Christmas has gone."*

They would not believe Santa was Santa.

Many people who were passing stopped to watch. Soon there was a crowd listening to this little old man who cried,

"I AM SANTA CLAUS."

Now, a policeman made his way through the crowd and asked, "What's the matter here?"

"There is a little old man," cried the children, "who says he is Santa Claus."

"Yes, Officer," said Santa, "I *am* Santa Claus."

"Is that so?" said the policeman. "Santa Claus, hey? Well, I think you had better come with me."

And he put his hand on Santa's shoulder and led him to police headquarters, followed by all the children.

"This little old man," said the policeman to the captain behind the desk, "pretends he is Santa Claus and is disturbing the peace in our street."

"That's bad," said the captain, with an especially deep policeman's voice. "We cannot allow this sort of thing in our town."

"But *I AM SANTA CLAUS*," shouted Santa Claus.

"No one can shout here but me," said the captain severely.

"Look, Captain Hooligan," began Santa, "I . . ."

"How do you know my name?" interrupted the captain.

"Santa knows everything," said Santa, "EVERYTHING. I can tell you what I dropped into your chimney last Christmas. There were blue pajamas for you, a wrist watch for your wife, Alice, and an electric train for your boy, Bobby. Do you believe I am Santa *now?*"

"Plum puddings and Easter eggs!" exclaimed the captain in astonishment. "That *is* what Santa left for us last Christmas."

"I also know, Captain," said Santa with a happy twinkle, "that you exchanged your blue pajamas for a pair with flowers on them."

"My wife liked the ones with flowers best," said the captain with a pink face.

"Then you should have flowers," said Santa. "Now I will show you again that Santa knows and remembers everything."

And he turned to the children who were crowded near the door and called them in, one by one, by their first names.

"This is Mary. I brought her a Dutch doll with a blue dress on Christmas day. Your doll has lost her wooden shoes, Mary. Look under the kitchen stove where the kitten was playing with them.

"This is William who paints such beautiful pictures with the paint box I gave him. Do not paint on the wallpaper, William.

"This is Ann. I left a stuffed polar bear for her, just like the real ones I see around my igloo.

"This is Dolly, who found a silver necklace in her sock.

"And Tommy, who got a baseball outfit.

"And Ted, and Nora, and Billy, and Jimmy . . ."

But no one was listening to Santa any more. All the children and the passers-by crowded around him and hugged and kissed him until his elegant felt hat was crushed flat on top of his head, and his fresh daffodil hung limp from his lapel.

"Dear old Santa . . . dear old Santa . . ." the captain and the policeman repeated tenderly over and over again.

After the hugging and kissing, they all went out for a stroll through the town to show Santa more of the gay Easter trimmings. And they took him through the stores where they bought piles of presents for him and for Mrs. Santa.

It was amidst a big cheering crowd that Santa finally left by plane for the airport far north where his sleigh was waiting. He was so happy, he was all smiles and twinkles.

Santa's sleigh had always left the North Pole full of gifts for others. But this time it was different. It was *returning* home filled with presents for Santa and Mrs. Santa. There were sugar Easter eggs, chocolate Easter eggs, plain eggs and decorated eggs, big eggs with small eggs inside, sugar bunnies and stuffed bunnies, a live white bunny with a yellow ribbon, cotton chicks and live chicks, bunches and bunches of daffodils, tulips, narcissus, and a beautiful Easter dress and a pretty flowered hat for Mrs. Santa.

Santa and Mrs. Santa had a very cheerful Easter indeed. Afterwards, when Santa went back to his toymaking, he knew that next Christmas he would load his sleigh with the most beautiful toys he had ever made.